THIS CANDLEWICK BOOK BELONGS TO:

_____

_____

_____

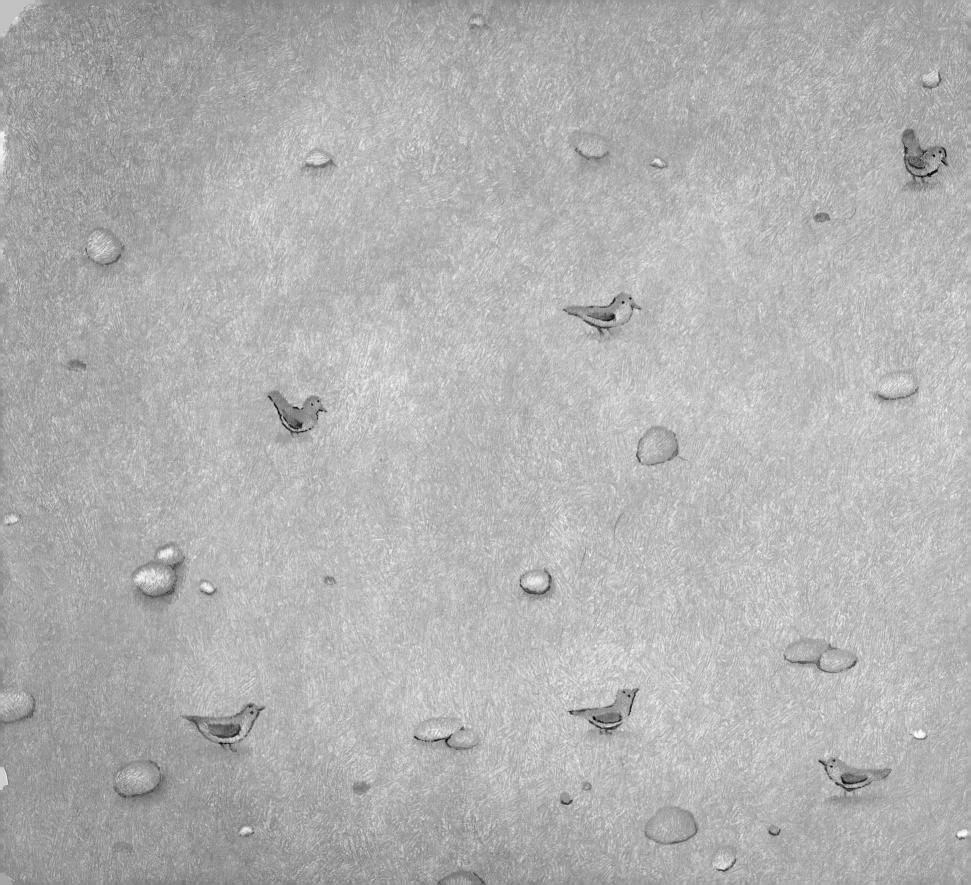

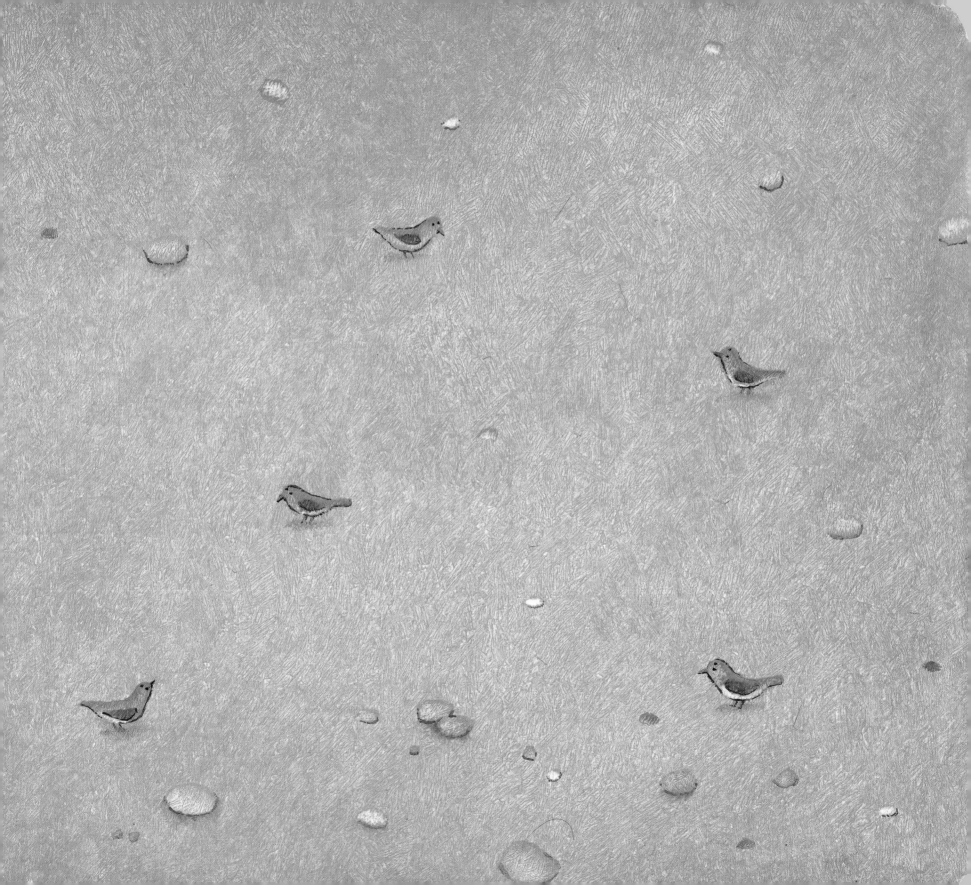

To librarians, who always know where to find things
P. R.

For Franny, who always knows where the moose is
R. C.

Text copyright © 2006 by Phyllis Root
Illustrations copyright © 2006 by Randy Cecil

First paperback edition 2008

The Library of Congress has cataloged the hardcover edition as follows:

Root, Phyllis.
Looking for a moose / Phyllis Root ; illustrated by Randy Cecil —1st ed.
p.  cm.
Summary: Four children set off into the woods to find a moose.
ISBN 978-0-7636-2005-9 (hardcover)
[1. Moose——Fiction. 2. Stories in rhyme.]  I. Cecil, Randy, ill. II. Title.
PZ8.3.R667Loo 2006
[E]——dc22     2006042581

ISBN 978-0-7636-3885-6 (paperback)

16 17 18 19 20 APS 14 13 12 11 10 9

Printed in Humen, Dongguan, China

This book was typeset in GothicBlond.
The illustrations were done in oil.

Candlewick Press
99 Dover Street
Somerville, Massachusetts 02144

visit us at www.candlewick.com

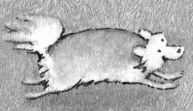

# Looking for a
# MOOSE

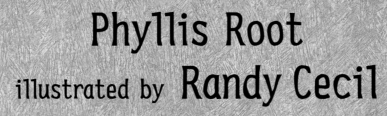

## Phyllis Root

## illustrated by Randy Cecil

CANDLEWICK PRESS

"Have you ever seen a moose—
a long-leggy moose—
a branchy-antler,
dinner-diving,
bulgy-nose
moose?"

"No! We've never, ever, ever, ever, ever seen a moose. And we really, really, really, really want to see a moose."

"Let's go!"
We put on our hats.
We pull on our boots.

We look in the woods—

**TROMP STOMP!**
**TROMP STOMP!**—

the treesy-breezy, tilty-stilty,
wobbly-knobbly woods.

We look and we look,
but it's just no use.
We don't see any long-leggy moose.
"Now what?"

"We'll look in the swamp
    for a dinner-diving moose!"
We roll up our pants.
    We take off our boots.

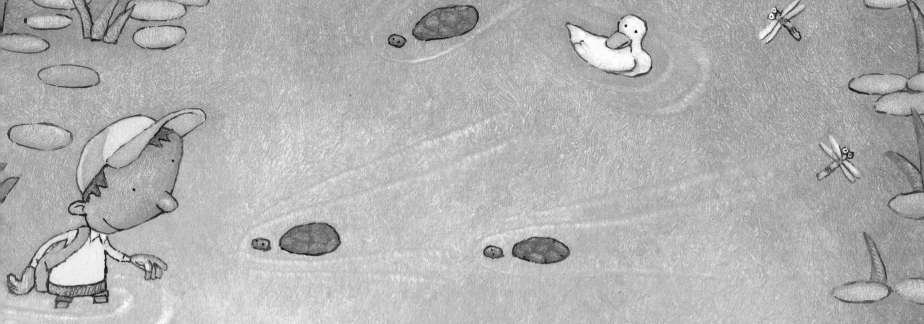

We wade in the swamp—

squeech squooch!
squeech squooch!—

the sloppy-gloppy, lily-loppy,
slurpy-glurpy swamp.

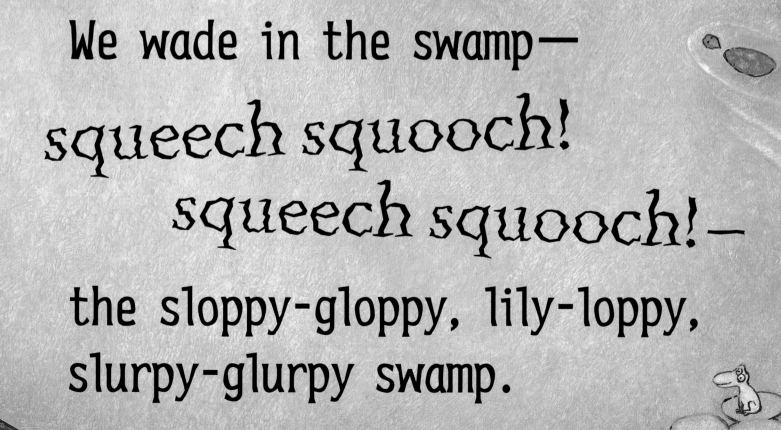

We look and we look,
    but it's just no use.
We don't see any long-leggy,
    dinner-diving moose.

"We'll look in the bushes for a branchy-antler moose!"

We roll down our pants.
We button up our sleeves.

We scrape through the bushes—

## scritch scratch!
### scritch scratch!—

the brambly-ambly, bunchy-scrunchy,
scrubby-shrubby bushes.

We look and we look,
but it's just no use.
We don't see any long-leggy,
dinner-diving,
branchy-antler moose.

"Now what?"

"We'll look on the hillside for
a bulgy-nose moose!"

We take off our hats.
We tighten up our packs.

We scramble up the hillside—
**TRIP TROP! TRIP TROP!**—
the rocky-blocky, lumpy-bumpy,
fuzzy-muzzy hillside.

We look and we look,
but it's just no use.
"We'll never, ever, ever, ever,
ever see a moose!"

"What's that?"

"LOOK THERE!
It's a long-leggy,
dinner-diving,
branchy-antler,
bulgy-nose moose . . .

and a moose . . .
    and a moose . . .

and a moose."

"We've never, ever, ever seen so many moose!"

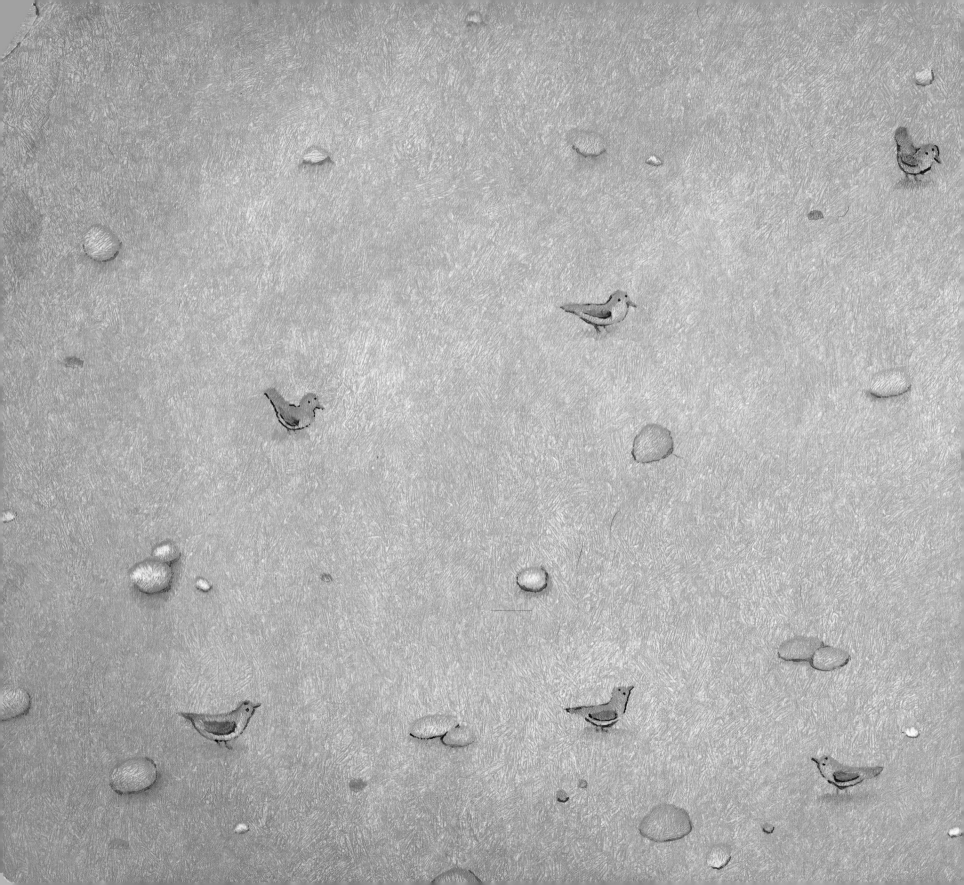

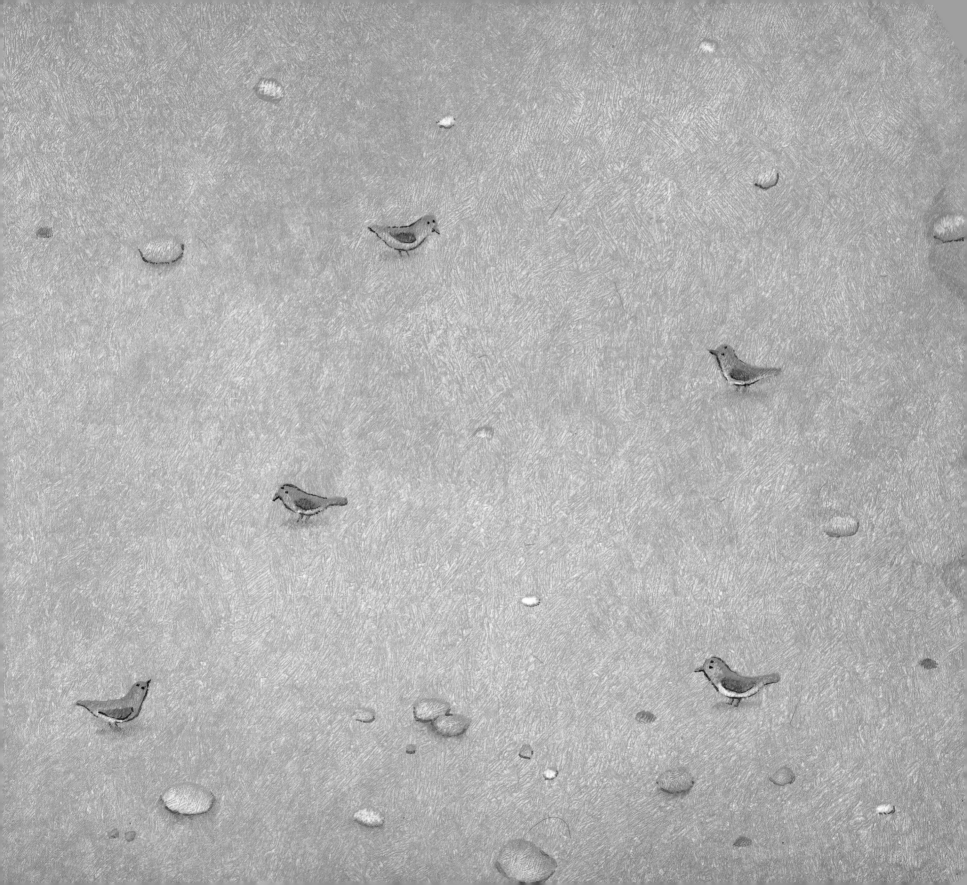

**Phyllis Root** says, "It's always a thrill to see a moose. One time when I was hiking on Isle Royale in Lake Superior, I came around a bend in the trail and was almost nose to muzzle with a bull moose. He was BIG. Luckily he was more interested in browsing than in me, so I was able to give him a wide bushwhacking berth and go on my way." Phyllis Root is the author of more than thirty books for children, including the *Boston Globe–Horn Book* Award-winning *Big Momma Makes the World*. She lives in Minneapolis.

**Randy Cecil** is the illustrator of many books for children, including the *New York Times* best-selling *And Here's to You!* by David Elliott, *We've All Got Bellybuttons!* by David Martin, and *My Father the Dog* by Elizabeth Bluemle. He is also the author-illustrator of the picture books *Gator* and *Duck,* among others. Randy Cecil lives in Houston.